CAMPING ADVENTURES
THIS JOURNAL BELONGS TO:

_____

Copyright © Aunt Meg and Me Journals

All Rights Reserved.

No portion of this book may be re-produced without the prior written permission of the publisher.

ISBN 9781097801978

How to Use This Journal

This journal is set-up to chronicle 3 separate week-long camping trips from start to finish. Alternatively, you can use the daily pages for shorter trips throughout the year. There are plenty of journal pages to cover 20+ weekend-long camping trips.

You don't have to go through the pages in order. **Feel free to jump around.** Write, doodle, draw, color or use stickers, pictures, leaves, maps, or anything else that holds a memory to capture the moment. **Have Fun!**

What is Included?

Before You Go
- Plan Your Camping Trip
- What Will You Take?
- What Will You Do?

Camp Activities
- Map Out Your Campsite
- Nature Treasure Hunt
- Camping Bingo

Daily Adventures
- Daily journal pages with prompts for writing about your adventures.
- Daily doodle pages for pictures, drawings, stickers and mementos.

GETTING READY

I AM GOING TO: _____

I AM GOING TO BE CAMPING FOR _____ DAYS.

COLOR IN THE DAYS YOU'LL BE CAMPING:

MONDAY	TUESDAY	WEDNESDAY	THURSDAY	FRIDAY	SATURDAY	SUNDAY
MONDAY	TUESDAY	WEDNESDAY	THURSDAY	FRIDAY	SATURDAY	SUNDAY
MONDAY	TUESDAY	WEDNESDAY	THURSDAY	FRIDAY	SATURDAY	SUNDAY

WHO IS GOING WITH ME:

LIST OTHER ITEMS YOU WANT TO REMEMBER TO PACK:

THINGS TO DO

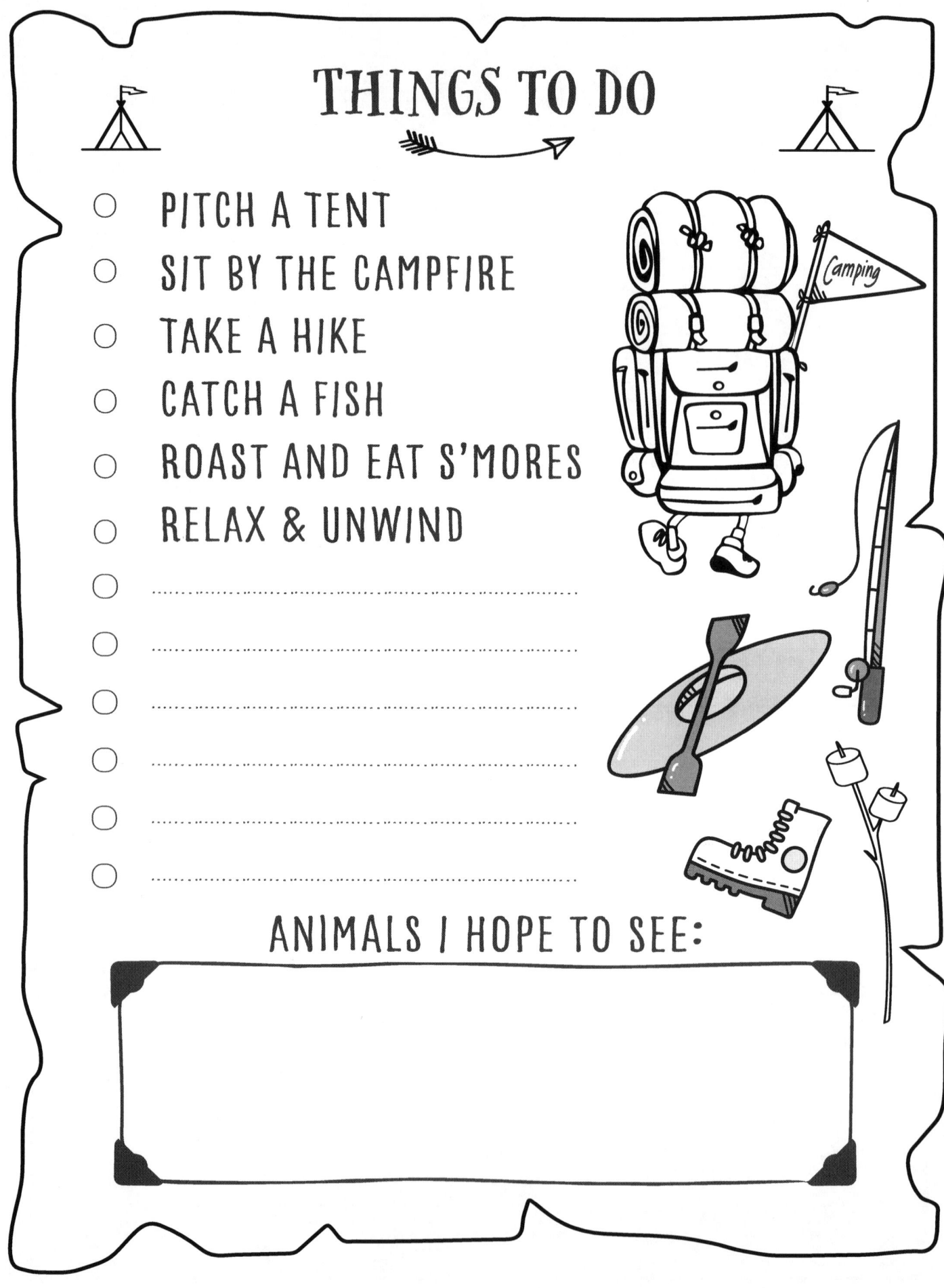

- ○ PITCH A TENT
- ○ SIT BY THE CAMPFIRE
- ○ TAKE A HIKE
- ○ CATCH A FISH
- ○ ROAST AND EAT S'MORES
- ○ RELAX & UNWIND
- ○ ....
- ○ ....
- ○ ....
- ○ ....
- ○ ....
- ○ ....

ANIMALS I HOPE TO SEE:

Safe Camping Rules

Stay Together

- STAY TOGETHER WITH YOUR GROUP.
- TELL A GROWN-UP YOUR LOCATION AT ALL TIMES.
- STAY ON THE MARKED TRAIL.
- ALWAYS WEAR YOUR WHISTLE, AND USE IT TO CALL FOR HELP IF YOU GET SEPARATED FROM YOUR GROUP.

Stay Healthy and Safe

- DON'T EAT ANY FRUITS OR PLANTS YOU FIND IN THE WILD BEFORE SHOWING IT TO A GROWN-UP.

- LEARN TO IDENTIFY COMMON POISONOUS PLANTS THAT MAY GROW IN YOUR CAMPING CLIMATE (SUCH AS POISON IVY AND POISON OAK). TAKE CARE TO AVOID THEM.

- WILD ANIMALS MAY LOOK CUTE AND CUDDLY, BUT NEVER TRY TO PET ONE.

- ASK YOUR CAMP LEADERS TO REVIEW FIRE SAFETY RULES EACH DAY. BE SURE TO PRACTICE THEM.

My Safe Camping Notes

_____

_____

_____

_____

_____

Things to watch-out for in our camping area:

Watch Out!

Plants	Animals

Locations	Situations

DRAW (OR ATTACH) A MAP OF THE CAMPSITE.

NATURE TREASURE HUNT

CAN YOU FIND?

- [ ] 2 ROCKS
- [ ] 1 LEAF
- [ ] 2 STICKS
- [ ] 3 FLOWERS
- [ ] 1 FEATHER
- [ ] 1 BARK
- [ ] 2 PINECONES
- [ ] 3 BERRIES

CAN YOU SEE?

- [ ] A BIRD
- [ ] A LIZARD
- [ ] A BUTTERFLY
- [ ] A DUCK
- [ ] AN INSECT
- [ ] A FISH

LOOK FOR SOMETHING WITH THE COLOR:

- [ ] GREEN
- [ ] YELLOW
- [ ] RED

Camping Selfie
SCAVENGER HUNT

GROUP SELFIE IN FRONT OF A LARGE TREE	GROUP SELFIE HOLDING PINE CONES	SELFIE WITH TWO KINDS OF STICKS
GROUP SELFIE ROASTING MARSHMALLOWS	GROUP SELFIE SITTING AROUND CAMP FIRE	GROUP SELFIE IN FRONT OF A LAKE
GROUP SELFIE IN FRONT OF A BOULDER	SELFIE STANDING ON A TREE STUMP	GROUP SELFIE IN FRONT OF A CAMP SIGN

Camping Awards

Funniest Moment

Best Activity

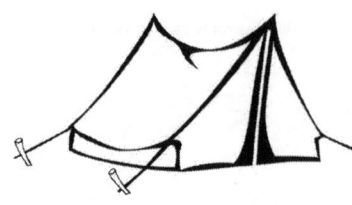

MY CAMPING ADVENTURES

CAMP NAME & LOCATION:　　　　　　　　　**DATE:**

TODAY'S ACTIVITIES

MY RATING OF TODAY

WEATHER REPORT

FAVORITE PART OF THE DAY

CAMPING BUDDIES

NOTES AND PICTURES

MY CAMPING ADVENTURES

ONE NEW THING I LEARNED TODAY:

BEST THING I ATE

THINGS I STILL WANT TO TRY TOMORROW OR NEXT TIME:

CAMPING DOODLES

WHAT I WANT TO REMEMBER MOST WHEN I GET BACK HOME:

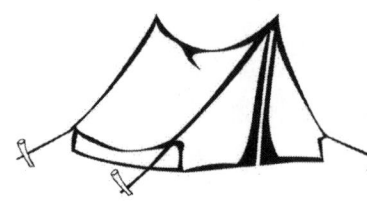

MY CAMPING ADVENTURES

CAMP NAME & LOCATION: _____ DATE: _____

TODAY'S ACTIVITIES

_____
_____
_____
_____

MY RATING OF TODAY

WEATHER REPORT

FAVORITE PART OF THE DAY

_____
_____
_____
_____
_____

CAMPING BUDDIES

NOTES AND PICTURES

CAMPING DOODLES

MY CAMPING ADVENTURES

ONE NEW THING I LEARNED TODAY:

BEST THING I ATE

THINGS I STILL WANT TO TRY TOMORROW OR NEXT TIME:

CAMPING DOODLES

WHAT I WANT TO REMEMBER MOST WHEN I GET BACK HOME:

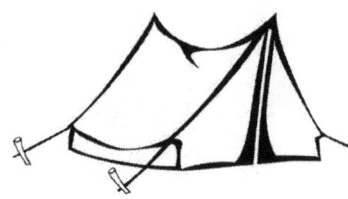

MY CAMPING ADVENTURES

CAMP NAME & LOCATION:

DATE:

TODAY'S ACTIVITIES

MY RATING OF TODAY

WEATHER REPORT

FAVORITE PART OF THE DAY

CAMPING BUDDIES

DOODLE OF ANIMALS I SAW

MY CAMPING ADVENTURES

ONE NEW THING I LEARNED TODAY:

BEST THING I ATE

CAMPING DOODLES

THINGS I STILL WANT TO TRY TOMORROW OR NEXT TIME:

WHAT I WANT TO REMEMBER MOST WHEN I GET BACK HOME:

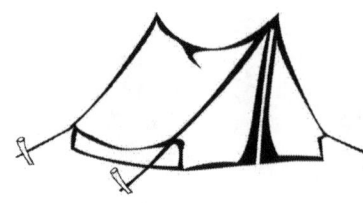

MY CAMPING ADVENTURES

CAMP NAME & LOCATION: _____ DATE: _____

TODAY'S ACTIVITIES

_____
_____
_____
_____
_____

MY RATING OF TODAY

WEATHER REPORT

FAVORITE PART OF THE DAY

_____
_____
_____
_____
_____

CAMPING BUDDIES

NOTES AND PICTURES

MY CAMPING ADVENTURES

ONE NEW THING I LEARNED TODAY:

BEST THING I ATE

THINGS I STILL WANT TO TRY TOMORROW OR NEXT TIME:

CAMPING DOODLES

WHAT I WANT TO REMEMBER MOST WHEN I GET BACK HOME:

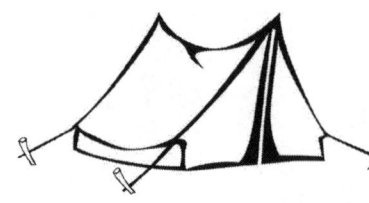

MY CAMPING ADVENTURES

CAMP NAME & LOCATION: DATE:

TODAY'S ACTIVITIES

MY RATING OF TODAY

WEATHER REPORT

FAVORITE PART OF THE DAY

CAMPING BUDDIES

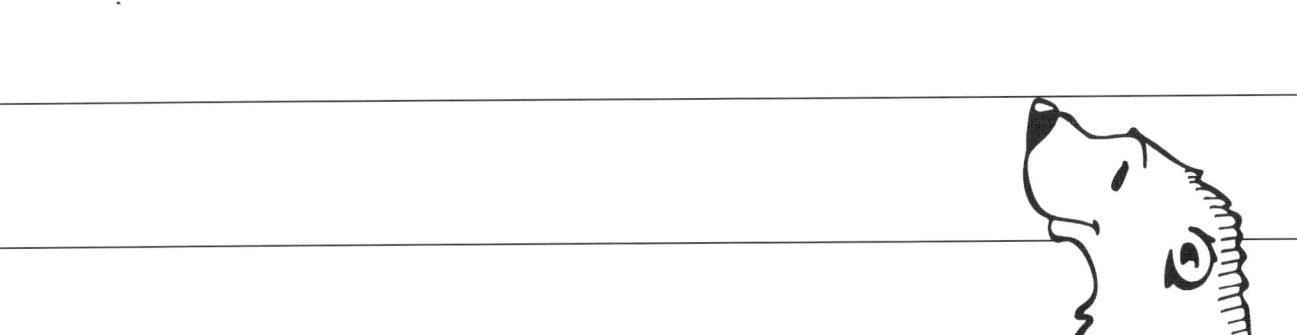

NOTES AND PICTURES

MY CAMPING ADVENTURES

ONE NEW THING I LEARNED TODAY:

BEST THING I ATE

CAMPING DOODLES

THINGS I STILL WANT TO TRY TOMORROW OR NEXT TIME:

WHAT I WANT TO REMEMBER MOST WHEN I GET BACK HOME:

MY CAMPING ADVENTURES

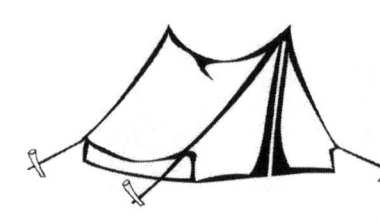

CAMP NAME & LOCATION: _____ **DATE:** _____

TODAY'S ACTIVITIES

MY RATING OF TODAY

WEATHER REPORT

FAVORITE PART OF THE DAY

CAMPING BUDDIES

DOODLE OF ANIMALS I SAW

NOTES AND PICTURES

MY CAMPING ADVENTURES

ONE NEW THING I LEARNED TODAY:

BEST THING I ATE

THINGS I STILL WANT TO TRY TOMORROW OR NEXT TIME:

CAMPING DOODLES

WHAT I WANT TO REMEMBER MOST WHEN I GET BACK HOME:

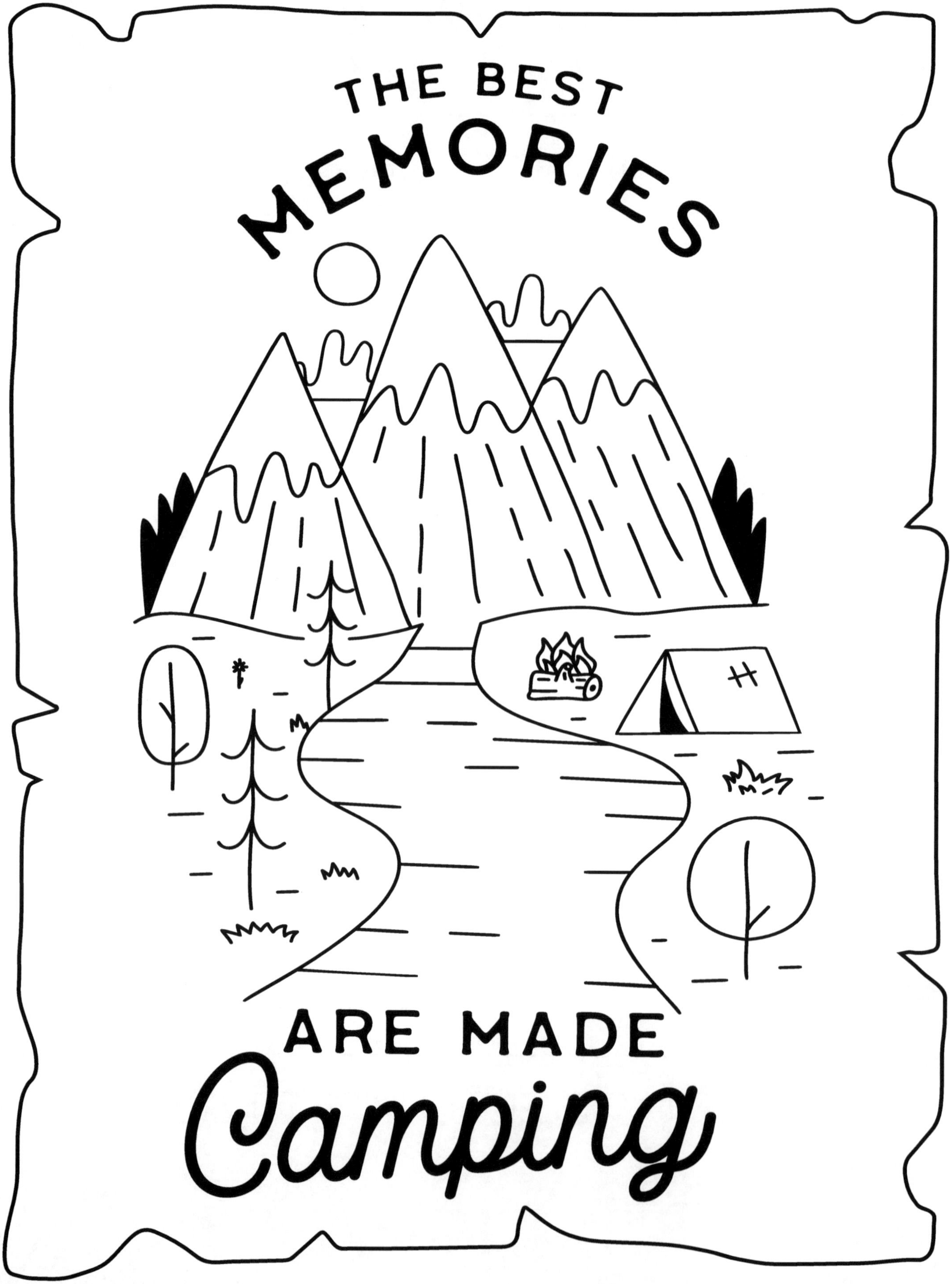
THE BEST
MEMORIES
ARE MADE
Camping

GETTING READY

I AM GOING TO: _____

I AM GOING TO BE CAMPING FOR ____ DAYS.

COLOR IN THE DAYS YOU'LL BE CAMPING:

MONDAY	TUESDAY	WEDNESDAY	THURSDAY	FRIDAY	SATURDAY	SUNDAY

MONDAY	TUESDAY	WEDNESDAY	THURSDAY	FRIDAY	SATURDAY	SUNDAY

MONDAY	TUESDAY	WEDNESDAY	THURSDAY	FRIDAY	SATURDAY	SUNDAY

WHO IS GOING WITH ME:

What Will You Take?

- FLASHLIGHT
- MAP OF CAMPSITE
- COMPASS
- HIKING BOOTS AND CLOTHES
- WATER
- CAMERA
- WHISTLE
- JOURNAL
- FIRST AID KIT
- SLEEPING BAG

LIST OTHER ITEMS YOU WANT TO REMEMBER TO PACK:

THINGS TO DO

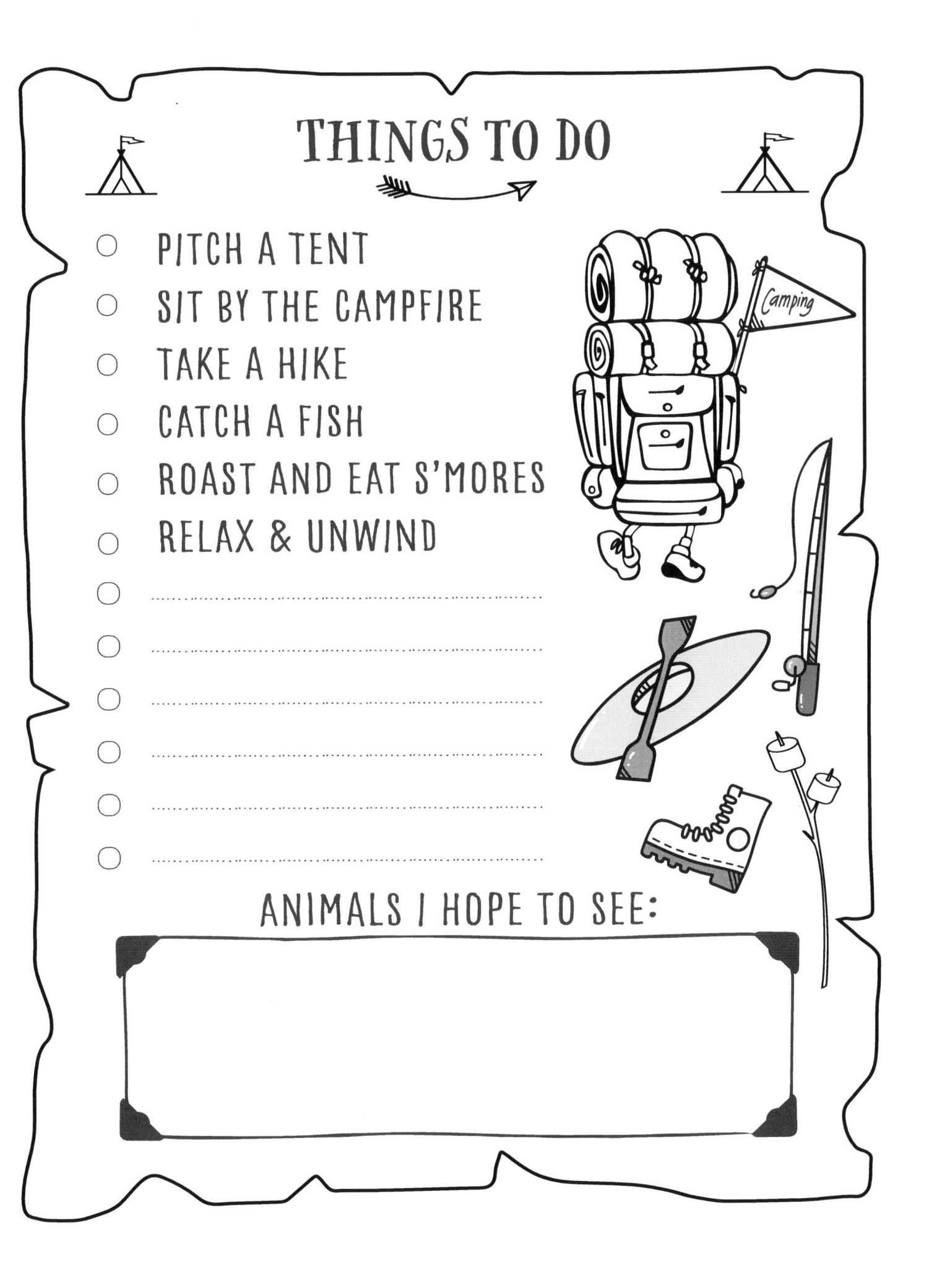

- ○ PITCH A TENT
- ○ SIT BY THE CAMPFIRE
- ○ TAKE A HIKE
- ○ CATCH A FISH
- ○ ROAST AND EAT S'MORES
- ○ RELAX & UNWIND
- ○ ....
- ○ ....
- ○ ....
- ○ ....
- ○ ....
- ○ ....

ANIMALS I HOPE TO SEE:

Safe Camping Rules

Stay Together

- STAY TOGETHER WITH YOUR GROUP.
- TELL A GROWN-UP YOUR LOCATION AT ALL TIMES.
- STAY ON THE MARKED TRAIL.
- ALWAYS WEAR YOUR WHISTLE, AND USE IT TO CALL FOR HELP IF YOU GET SEPARATED FROM YOUR GROUP.

Stay Healthy and Safe

- DON'T EAT ANY FRUITS OR PLANTS YOU FIND IN THE WILD BEFORE SHOWING IT TO A GROWN-UP.
- LEARN TO IDENTIFY COMMON POISONOUS PLANTS THAT MAY GROW IN YOUR CAMPING CLIMATE (SUCH AS POISON IVY AND POISON OAK). TAKE CARE TO AVOID THEM.
- WILD ANIMALS MAY LOOK CUTE AND CUDDLY, BUT NEVER TRY TO PET ONE.
- ASK YOUR CAMP LEADERS TO REVIEW FIRE SAFETY RULES EACH DAY. BE SURE TO PRACTICE THEM.

My Safe Camping Notes

_____

_____

_____

_____

Things to watch-out for in our camping area:

Watch Out!

Plants	Animals

Locations	Situations

DRAW (OR ATTACH) A MAP OF THE CAMPSITE.

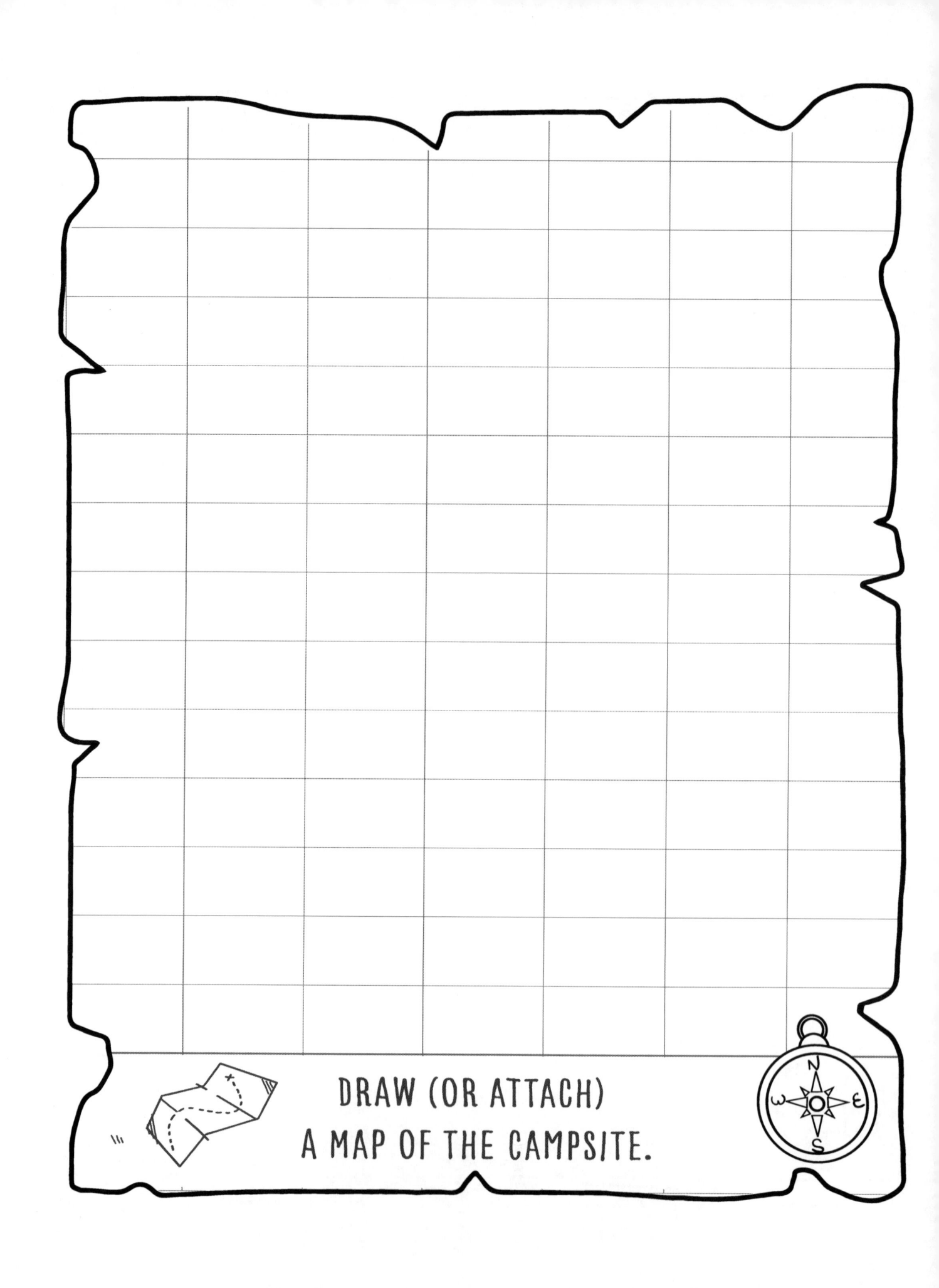

camping Bingo

GET FOUR IN A ROW, UP, DOWN OR ACROSS, TO WIN

CAMPER	HOT COCOA	FLASHLIGHT	FROG
CAMP FIRE	TENT	MUSHROOMS	BINOCULAR
AXE	LIZARD	COMPASS	FISHING POLE
FISH	LOG	MARSHMALLOW FOR S'MORES	LANTERN

Camping Bingo

GET FOUR IN A ROW, UP, DOWN OR ACROSS, TO WIN

PINE TREE	TREE STUMP	OWL	AXE
FLASHLIGHT	CAMP SIGN	ACORN	CAMP FIRE
BINOCULAR	HIKING BOOT	MAPLE LEAF	CANOE
COMPASS	TENT	SQUIRREL	GRILL

NATURE TREASURE HUNT

CAN YOU FIND?

- ☐ 2 ROCKS
- ☐ 1 LEAF
- ☐ 2 STICKS
- ☐ 3 FLOWERS
- ☐ 1 FEATHER
- ☐ 1 BARK
- ☐ 2 PINECONES
- ☐ 3 BERRIES

CAN YOU SEE?

- ☐ A BIRD
- ☐ A LIZARD
- ☐ A BUTTERFLY
- ☐ A DUCK
- ☐ AN INSECT
- ☐ A FISH

LOOK FOR SOMETHING WITH THE COLOR:

- ☐ GREEN
- ☐ YELLOW
- ☐ RED

Camping Selfie
SCAVENGER HUNT

GROUP SELFIE IN FRONT OF A LARGE TREE	GROUP SELFIE HOLDING PINE CONES	SELFIE WITH TWO KINDS OF STICKS
GROUP SELFIE ROASTING MARSHMALLOWS	GROUP SELFIE SITTING AROUND CAMP FIRE	GROUP SELFIE IN FRONT OF A LAKE
GROUP SELFIE IN FRONT OF A BOULDER	SELFIE STANDING ON A TREE STUMP	GROUP SELFIE IN FRONT OF A CAMP SIGN

Camping Awards

First Up In The Morning

Last Up In The Morning

Marshmallow Master

Best Cook

Best Campfire Story

Camping Awards

Funniest Moment

Best Activity

MY CAMPING ADVENTURES

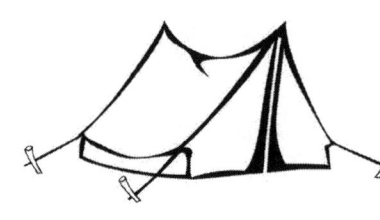

CAMP NAME & LOCATION: _____ **DATE:** _____

TODAY'S ACTIVITIES

_____
_____
_____
_____
_____

MY RATING OF TODAY

WEATHER REPORT

FAVORITE PART OF THE DAY

_____
_____
_____
_____
_____

CAMPING BUDDIES

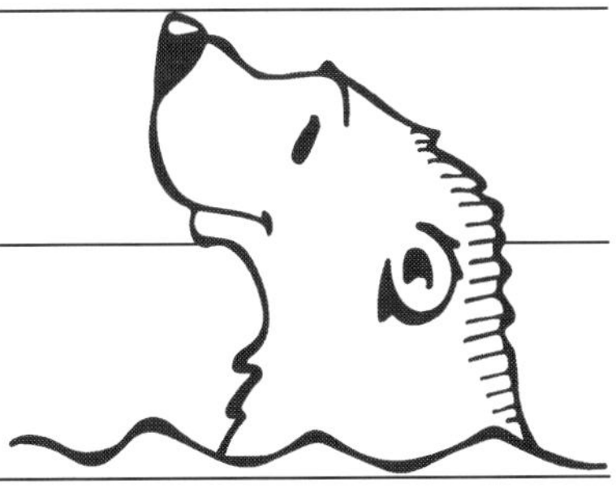

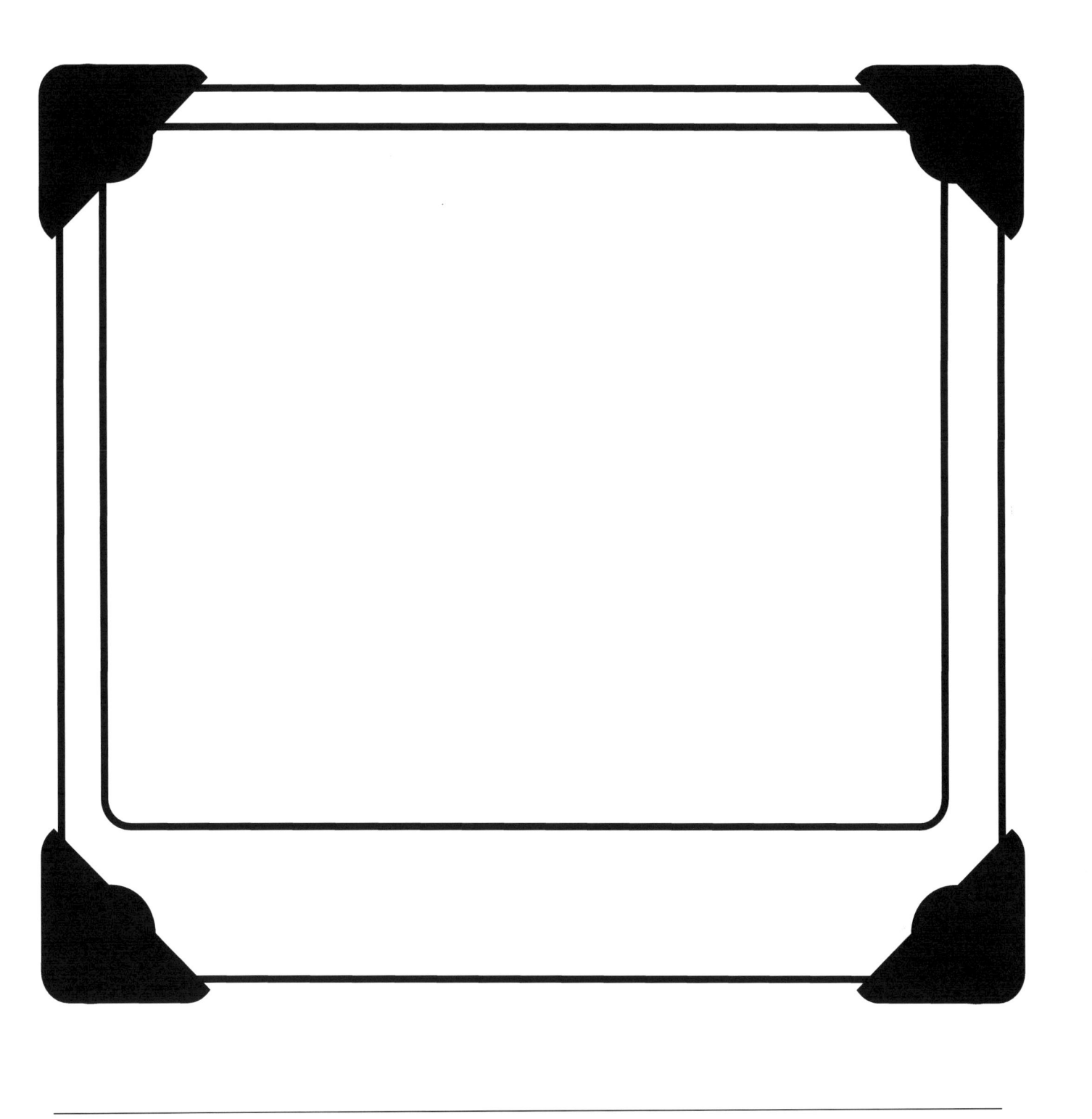

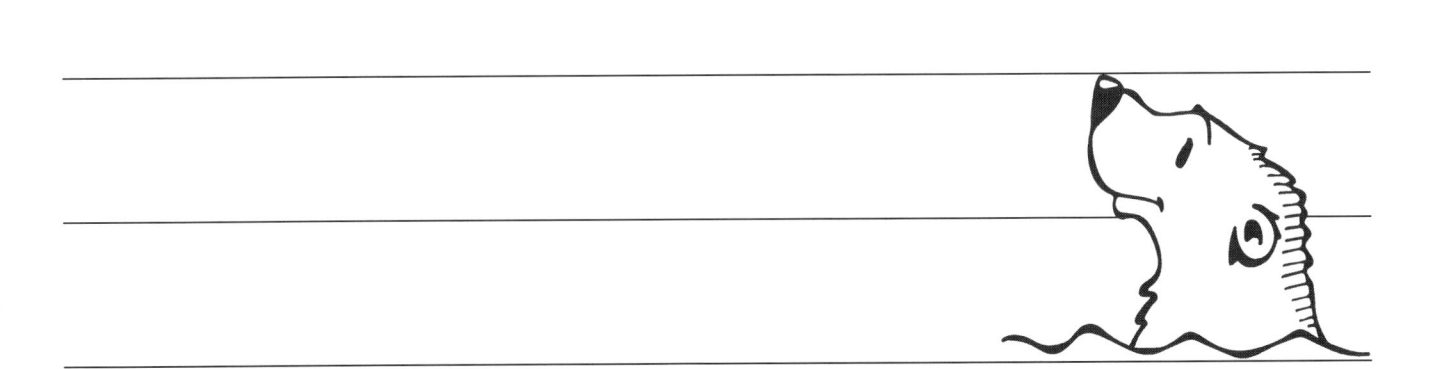

NOTES AND PICTURES

MY CAMPING ADVENTURES

ONE NEW THING I LEARNED TODAY:

BEST THING I ATE

CAMPING DOODLES

THINGS I STILL WANT TO TRY TOMORROW OR NEXT TIME:

WHAT I WANT TO REMEMBER MOST WHEN I GET BACK HOME:

MY CAMPING ADVENTURES

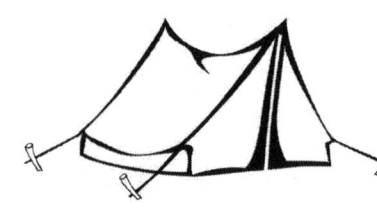

CAMP NAME & LOCATION: _____ **DATE:** _____

TODAY'S ACTIVITIES

_____
_____
_____
_____

MY RATING OF TODAY

WEATHER REPORT

FAVORITE PART OF THE DAY

_____
_____
_____
_____

CAMPING BUDDIES

NOTES AND PICTURES

CAMPING DOODLES

MY CAMPING ADVENTURES

ONE NEW THING I LEARNED TODAY:

BEST THING I ATE

THINGS I STILL WANT TO TRY TOMORROW OR NEXT TIME:

CAMPING DOODLES

WHAT I WANT TO REMEMBER MOST WHEN I GET BACK HOME:

MY CAMPING ADVENTURES

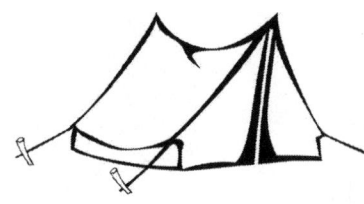

CAMP NAME & LOCATION: DATE:

TODAY'S ACTIVITIES

MY RATING OF TODAY

WEATHER REPORT

FAVORITE PART OF THE DAY

CAMPING BUDDIES

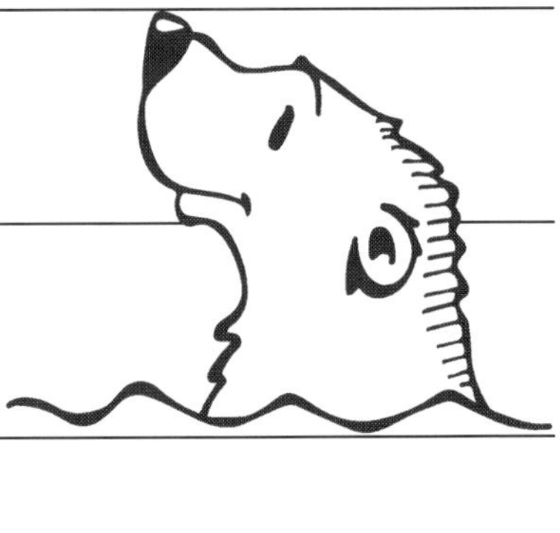

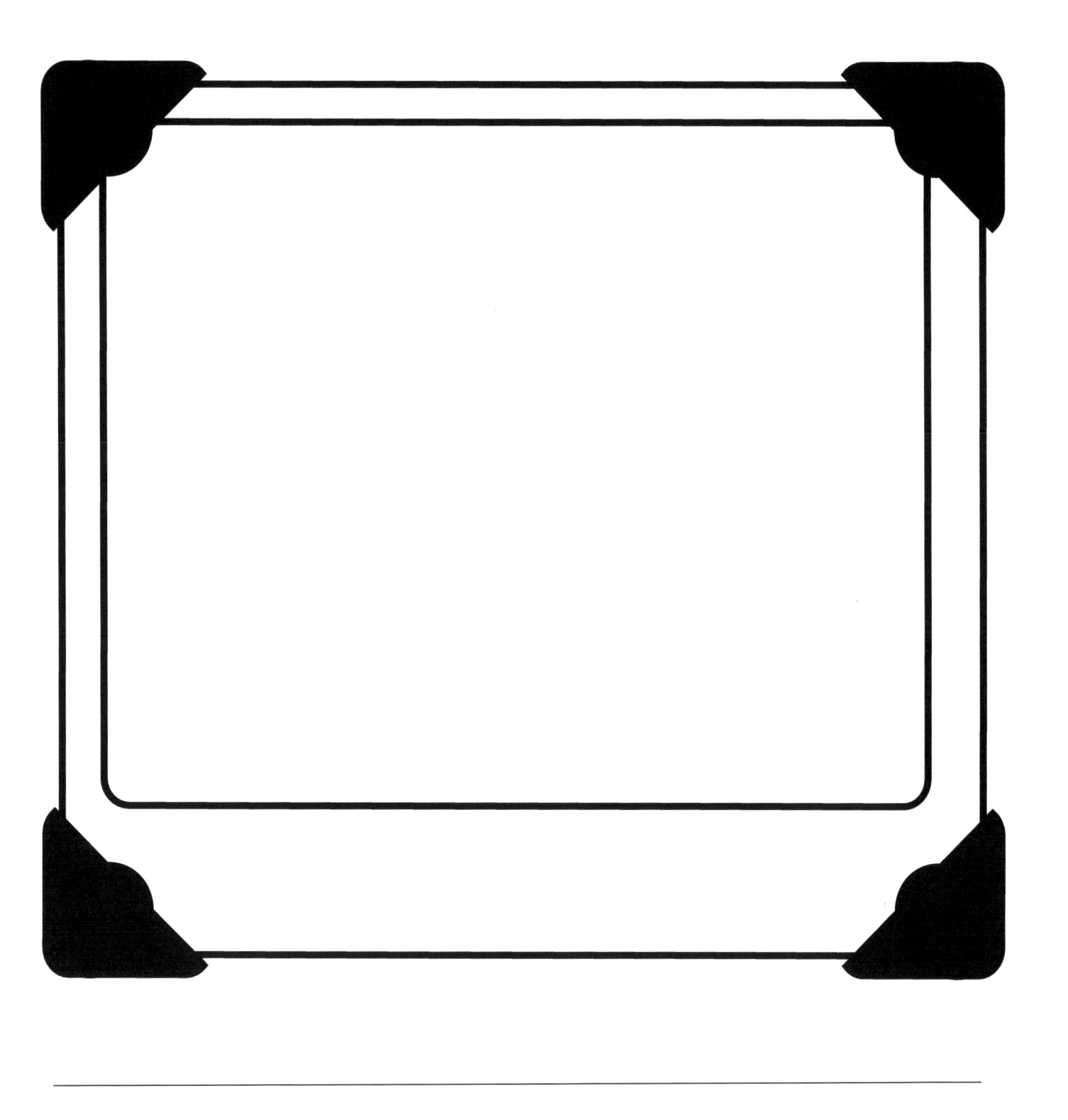

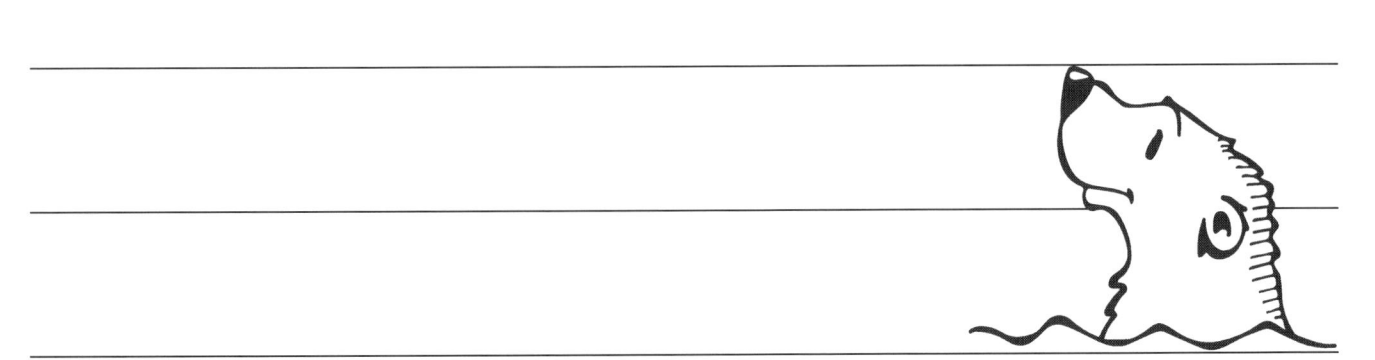

DOODLE OF ANIMALS I SAW

MY CAMPING ADVENTURES

ONE NEW THING I LEARNED TODAY:

BEST THING I ATE

CAMPING DOODLES

THINGS I STILL WANT TO TRY TOMORROW OR NEXT TIME:

WHAT I WANT TO REMEMBER MOST WHEN I GET BACK HOME:

MY CAMPING ADVENTURES

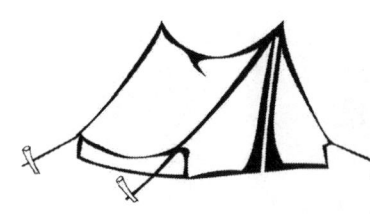

CAMP NAME & LOCATION: _____ **DATE:** _____

TODAY'S ACTIVITIES

_____
_____
_____
_____
_____

MY RATING OF TODAY

★ ★ ★ ★ ★

WEATHER REPORT

FAVORITE PART OF THE DAY

_____
_____
_____
_____
_____

CAMPING BUDDIES

CAMPING DOODLES

NOTES AND PICTURES

MY CAMPING ADVENTURES

ONE NEW THING I LEARNED TODAY:

BEST THING I ATE

CAMPING DOODLES

THINGS I STILL WANT TO TRY TOMORROW OR NEXT TIME:

WHAT I WANT TO REMEMBER MOST WHEN I GET BACK HOME:

MY CAMPING ADVENTURES

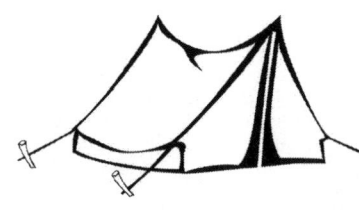

CAMP NAME & LOCATION:

DATE:

TODAY'S ACTIVITIES

MY RATING OF TODAY

WEATHER REPORT

FAVORITE PART OF THE DAY

CAMPING BUDDIES

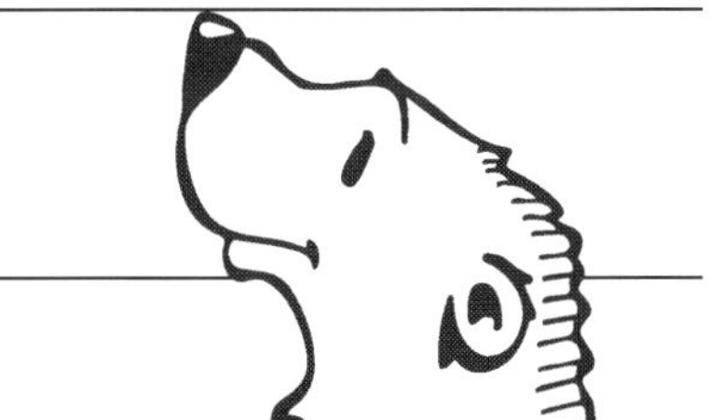

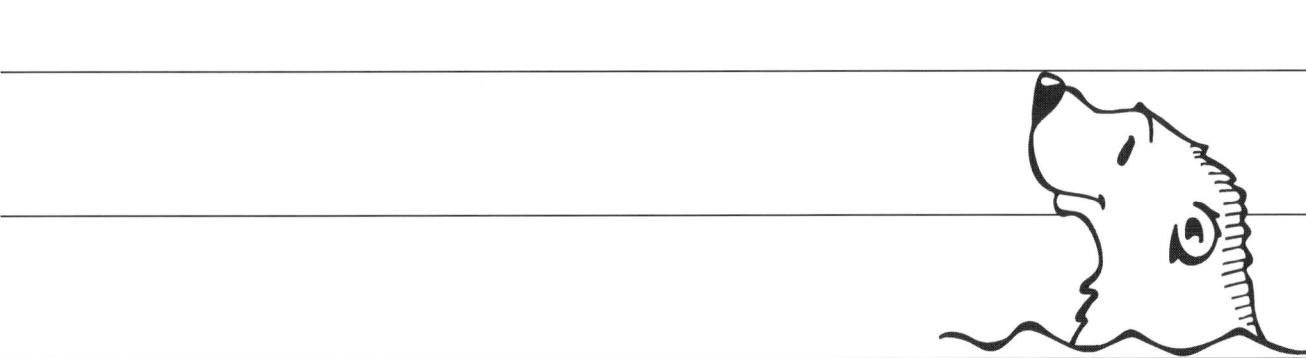

NOTES AND PICTURES

MY CAMPING ADVENTURES

ONE NEW THING I LEARNED TODAY:

BEST THING I ATE

THINGS I STILL WANT TO TRY TOMORROW OR NEXT TIME:

CAMPING DOODLES

WHAT I WANT TO REMEMBER MOST WHEN I GET BACK HOME:

MY CAMPING ADVENTURES

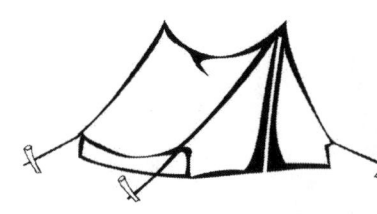

CAMP NAME & LOCATION: _____ **DATE:** _____

TODAY'S ACTIVITIES

_____
_____
_____
_____

MY RATING OF TODAY

WEATHER REPORT

FAVORITE PART OF THE DAY

_____
_____
_____
_____

CAMPING BUDDIES

DOODLE OF ANIMALS I SAW

NOTES AND PICTURES

MY CAMPING ADVENTURES

ONE NEW THING I LEARNED TODAY:

BEST THING I ATE

CAMPING DOODLES

THINGS I STILL WANT TO TRY TOMORROW OR NEXT TIME:

WHAT I WANT TO REMEMBER MOST WHEN I GET BACK HOME:

THE BEST MEMORIES ARE MADE *Camping*

GETTING READY

I AM GOING TO:

I AM GOING TO BE CAMPING FOR ☐ DAYS.

COLOR IN THE DAYS YOU'LL BE CAMPING:

MONDAY	TUESDAY	WEDNESDAY	THURSDAY	FRIDAY	SATURDAY	SUNDAY

MONDAY	TUESDAY	WEDNESDAY	THURSDAY	FRIDAY	SATURDAY	SUNDAY

MONDAY	TUESDAY	WEDNESDAY	THURSDAY	FRIDAY	SATURDAY	SUNDAY

WHO IS GOING WITH ME:

WHAT WILL YOU TAKE?

- FLASHLIGHT
- MAP OF CAMPSITE
- COMPASS
- HIKING BOOTS AND CLOTHES
- WATER
- CAMERA
- WHISTLE
- JOURNAL
- FIRST AID KIT
- SLEEPING BAG

LIST OTHER ITEMS YOU WANT TO REMEMBER TO PACK:

THINGS TO DO

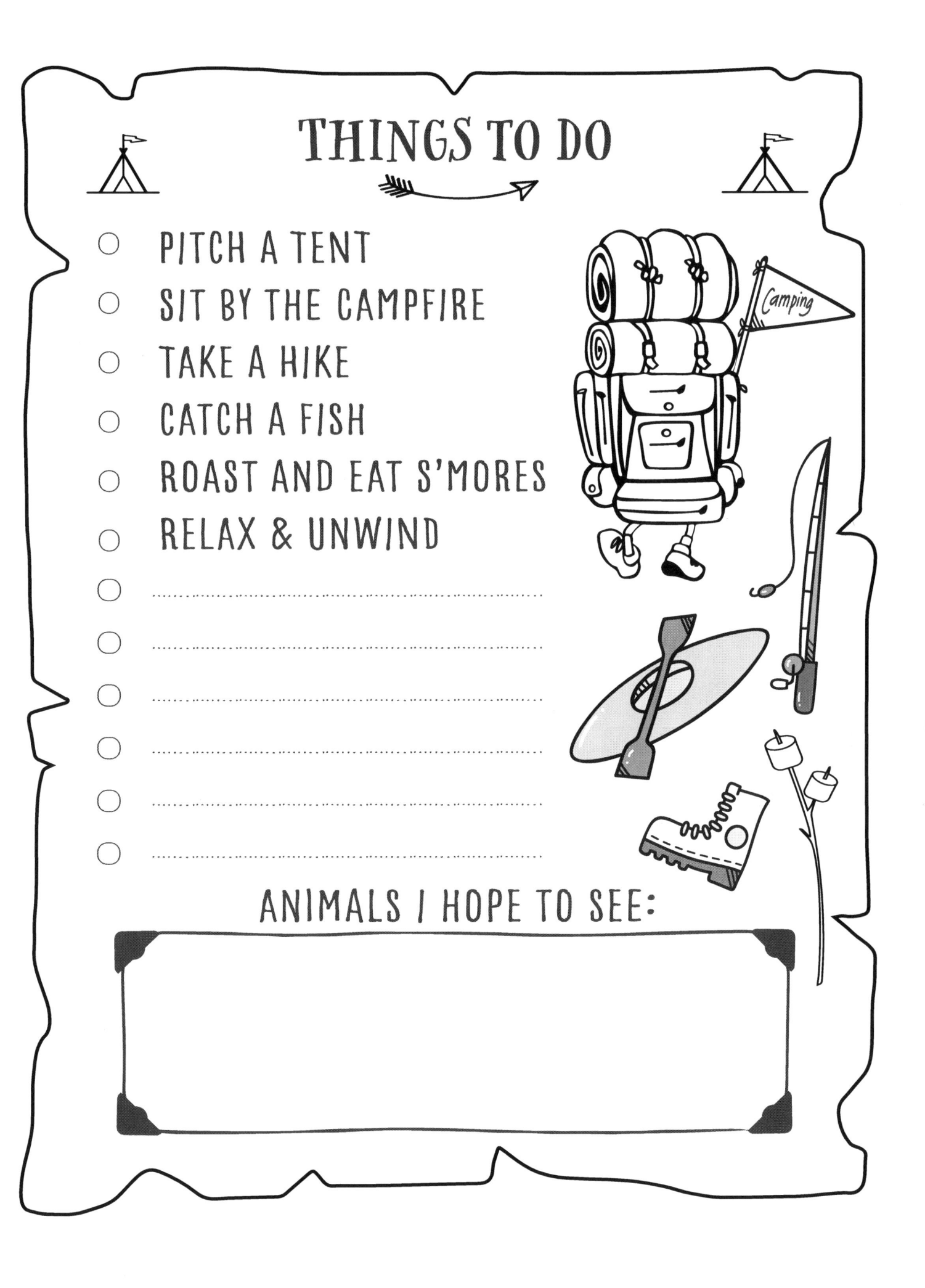

- ○ PITCH A TENT
- ○ SIT BY THE CAMPFIRE
- ○ TAKE A HIKE
- ○ CATCH A FISH
- ○ ROAST AND EAT S'MORES
- ○ RELAX & UNWIND
- ○ ....
- ○ ....
- ○ ....
- ○ ....
- ○ ....
- ○ ....

ANIMALS I HOPE TO SEE:

Safe Camping Rules

Stay Together

- Stay together with your group.
- Tell a grown-up your location at all times.
- Stay on the marked trail.
- Always wear your whistle, and use it to call for help if you get separated from your group.

Stay Healthy and Safe

- Don't eat any fruits or plants you find in the wild before showing it to a grown-up.
- Learn to identify common poisonous plants that may grow in your camping climate (such as poison ivy and poison oak). Take care to avoid them.
- Wild animals may look cute and cuddly, but never try to pet one.
- Ask your camp leaders to review fire safety rules each day. Be sure to practice them.

My Safe Camping Notes

_____

_____

_____

_____

_____

Things to watch-out for in our camping area:

Watch Out!

Plants	Animals

Locations	Situations

DRAW (OR ATTACH) A MAP OF THE CAMPSITE.

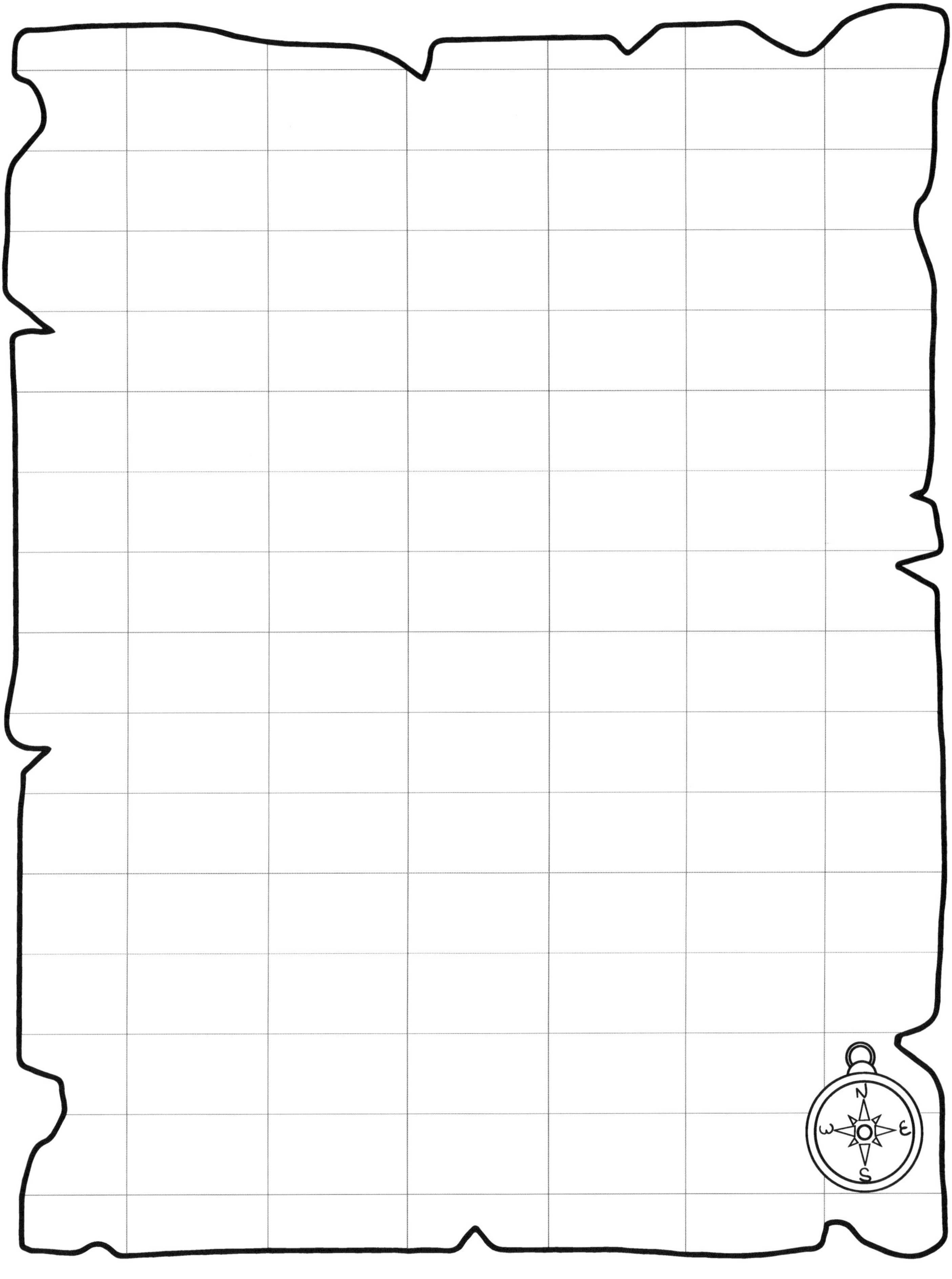
N
S

Camping Bingo

GET FOUR IN A ROW, UP, DOWN OR ACROSS, TO WIN

CAMPER	HOT COCOA	FLASHLIGHT	FROG
CAMP FIRE	TENT	MUSHROOMS	BINOCULAR
AXE	LIZARD	COMPASS	FISHING POLE
FISH	LOG	MARSHMALLOW FOR S'MORES	LANTERN

Camping Bingo

GET FOUR IN A ROW, UP, DOWN OR ACROSS, TO WIN

PINE TREE	TREE STUMP	OWL	AXE
FLASHLIGHT	CAMP SIGN	ACORN	CAMP FIRE
BINOCULAR	HIKING BOOT	MAPLE LEAF	CANOE
COMPASS	TENT	SQUIRREL	GRILL

NATURE TREASURE HUNT

CAN YOU FIND?

- ☐ 2 ROCKS
- ☐ 1 LEAF
- ☐ 2 STICKS
- ☐ 3 FLOWERS
- ☐ 1 FEATHER
- ☐ 1 BARK
- ☐ 2 PINECONES
- ☐ 3 BERRIES

CAN YOU SEE?

- ☐ A BIRD
- ☐ A LIZARD
- ☐ A BUTTERFLY
- ☐ A DUCK
- ☐ AN INSECT
- ☐ A FISH

LOOK FOR SOMETHING WITH THE COLOR:

- ☐ GREEN
- ☐ YELLOW
- ☐ RED

Camping Selfie
SCAVENGER HUNT

GROUP SELFIE IN FRONT OF A LARGE TREE	GROUP SELFIE HOLDING PINE CONES	SELFIE WITH TWO KINDS OF STICKS
GROUP SELFIE ROASTING MARSHMALLOWS	GROUP SELFIE SITTING AROUND CAMP FIRE	GROUP SELFIE IN FRONT OF A LAKE
GROUP SELFIE IN FRONT OF A BOULDER	SELFIE STANDING ON A TREE STUMP	GROUP SELFIE IN FRONT OF A CAMP SIGN

Camping Awards

First Up In The Morning

Last Up In The Morning

Marshmallow Master

Best Cook

Best Campfire Story

Camping Awards

Funniest Moment

....

Best Activity

....

MY CAMPING ADVENTURES

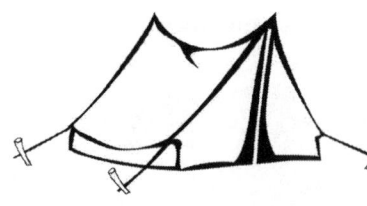

CAMP NAME & LOCATION: _____ **DATE:** _____

TODAY'S ACTIVITIES

MY RATING OF TODAY
☆ ☆ ☆ ☆ ☆

_____
_____
_____
_____
_____

WEATHER REPORT

FAVORITE PART OF THE DAY

CAMPING BUDDIES

_____
_____
_____
_____
_____

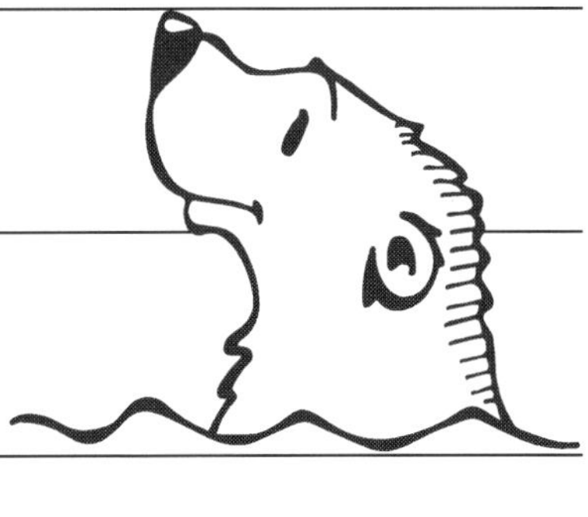

NOTES AND PICTURES

MY CAMPING ADVENTURES

ONE NEW THING I LEARNED TODAY:

BEST THING I ATE

CAMPING DOODLES

THINGS I STILL WANT TO TRY TOMORROW OR NEXT TIME:

WHAT I WANT TO REMEMBER MOST WHEN I GET BACK HOME:

MY CAMPING ADVENTURES

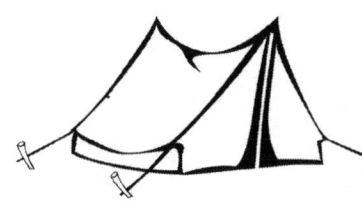

CAMP NAME & LOCATION:

DATE:

TODAY'S ACTIVITIES

MY RATING OF TODAY

WEATHER REPORT

FAVORITE PART OF THE DAY

CAMPING BUDDIES

NOTES AND PICTURES

CAMPING DOODLES

MY CAMPING ADVENTURES

ONE NEW THING I LEARNED TODAY:

BEST THING I ATE

CAMPING DOODLES

THINGS I STILL WANT TO TRY TOMORROW OR NEXT TIME:

WHAT I WANT TO REMEMBER MOST WHEN I GET BACK HOME:

MY CAMPING ADVENTURES

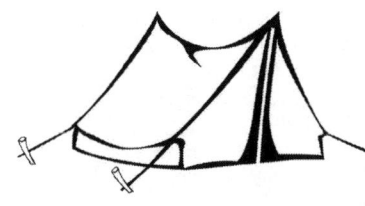

CAMP NAME & LOCATION:

DATE:

TODAY'S ACTIVITIES

MY RATING OF TODAY

WEATHER REPORT

FAVORITE PART OF THE DAY

CAMPING BUDDIES

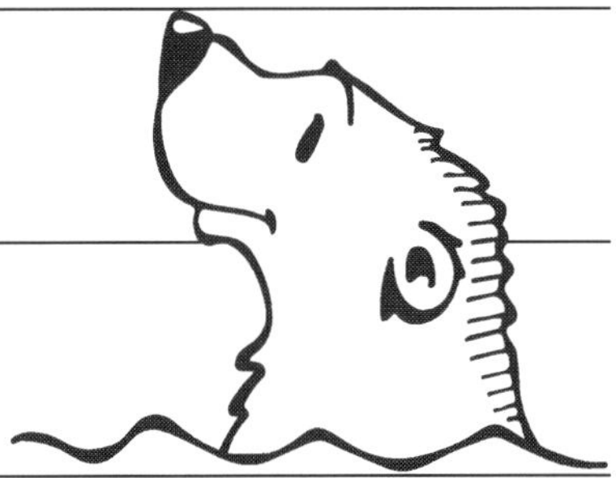

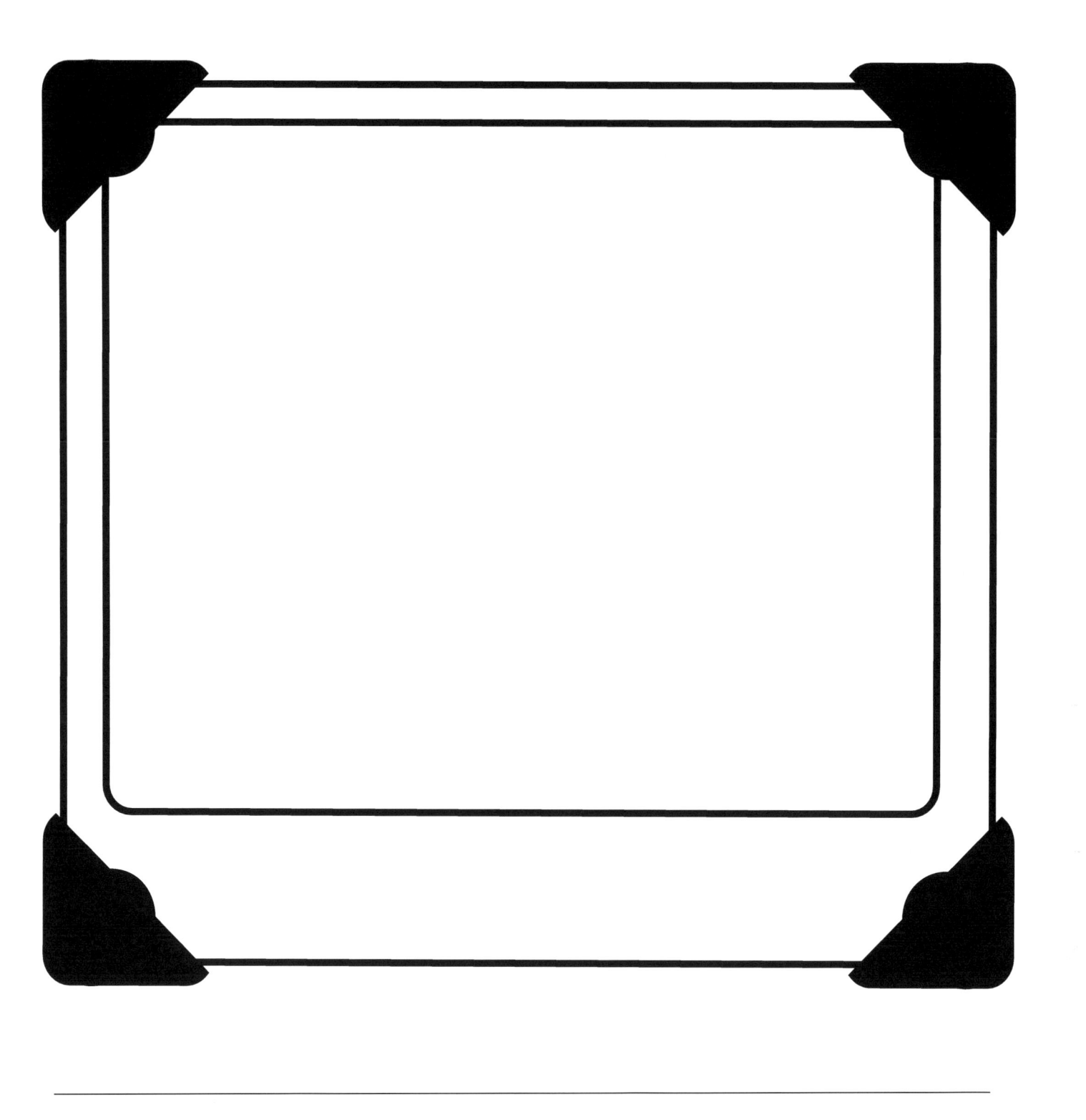

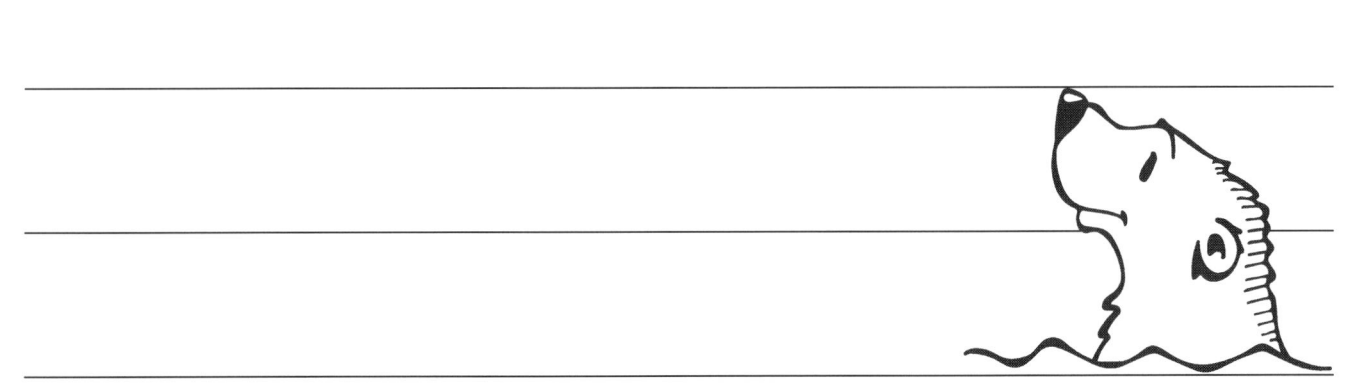

DOODLE OF ANIMALS I SAW

MY CAMPING ADVENTURES

ONE NEW THING I LEARNED TODAY:

BEST THING I ATE

CAMPING DOODLES

THINGS I STILL WANT TO TRY TOMORROW OR NEXT TIME:

WHAT I WANT TO REMEMBER MOST WHEN I GET BACK HOME:

MY CAMPING ADVENTURES

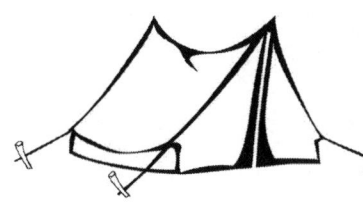

CAMP NAME & LOCATION:

DATE:

TODAY'S ACTIVITIES

MY RATING OF TODAY

WEATHER REPORT

FAVORITE PART OF THE DAY

CAMPING BUDDIES

CAMPING DOODLES

NOTES AND PICTURES

MY CAMPING ADVENTURES

ONE NEW THING I LEARNED TODAY:

BEST THING I ATE

CAMPING DOODLES

THINGS I STILL WANT TO TRY TOMORROW OR NEXT TIME:

WHAT I WANT TO REMEMBER MOST WHEN I GET BACK HOME:

MY CAMPING ADVENTURES

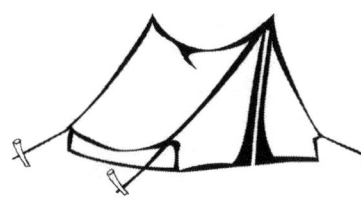

CAMP NAME & LOCATION: _____ **DATE:** _____

TODAY'S ACTIVITIES

_____
_____
_____
_____
_____
_____

MY RATING OF TODAY

WEATHER REPORT

FAVORITE PART OF THE DAY

_____
_____
_____
_____
_____
_____

CAMPING BUDDIES

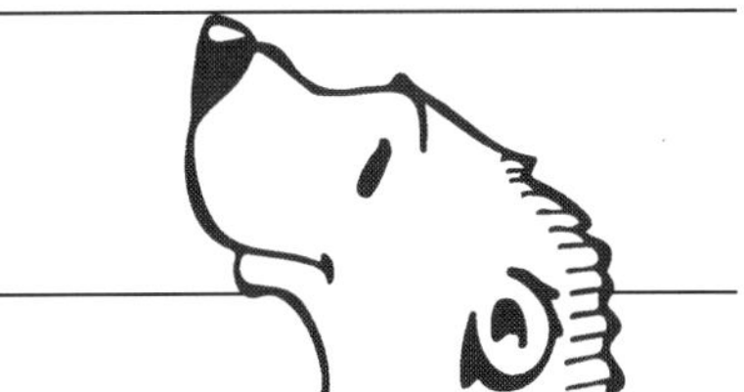

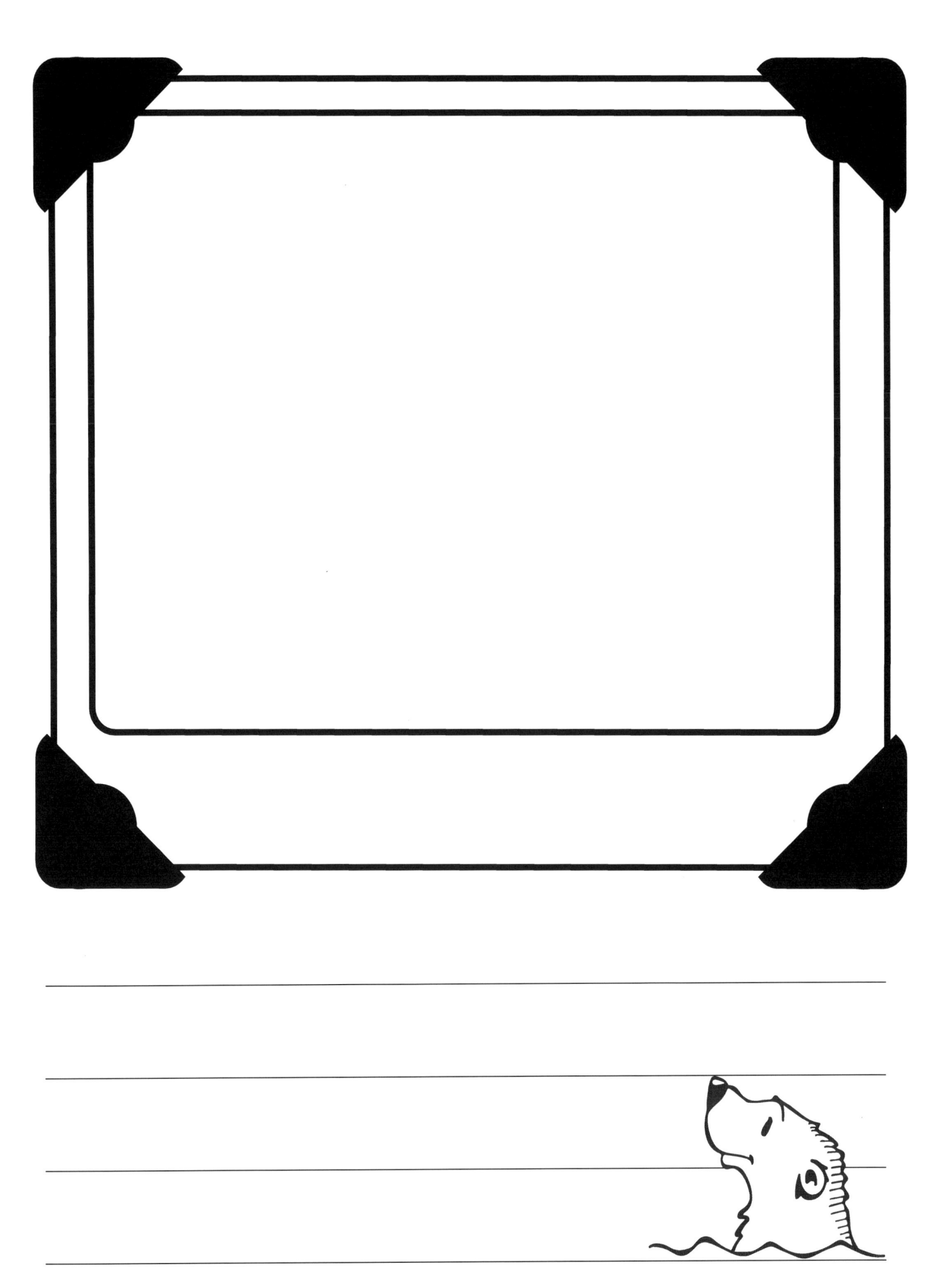

NOTES AND PICTURES

MY CAMPING ADVENTURES

ONE NEW THING I LEARNED TODAY:

BEST THING I ATE

CAMPING DOODLES

THINGS I STILL WANT TO TRY TOMORROW OR NEXT TIME:

WHAT I WANT TO REMEMBER MOST WHEN I GET BACK HOME:

MY CAMPING ADVENTURES

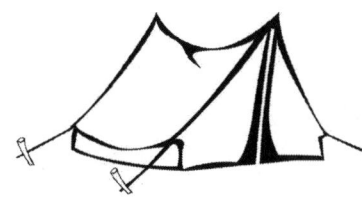

CAMP NAME & LOCATION: _____   DATE: _____

TODAY'S ACTIVITIES

MY RATING OF TODAY

_____
_____
_____
_____
_____

WEATHER REPORT

FAVORITE PART OF THE DAY

CAMPING BUDDIES

_____
_____
_____
_____
_____

DOODLE OF ANIMALS I SAW

NOTES AND PICTURES

MY CAMPING ADVENTURES

ONE NEW THING I LEARNED TODAY:

BEST THING I ATE

CAMPING DOODLES

THINGS I STILL WANT TO TRY TOMORROW OR NEXT TIME:

WHAT I WANT TO REMEMBER MOST WHEN I GET BACK HOME:

ADVENTURE IS WAITING

Made in the USA
Columbia, SC
03 July 2025